Pia the Pinena Fairy

The Legendary
Judges of Magic

Written & Illustrated by

Amy Zhao

This is a fiction story.
Names and places in this book are the
product of the author's imagination or
used fictitiously. It is pure coincidental if
they resemble any actual thing.

This book is dedicated to all my wonderful teachers.

From my delightful Sunrise Elementary:

> Ms. Herron, there's some amazing magic within you that attracts us to your class like a magnet.
> Ms. Billes, your love for the students will be with us forever.
> Ms. Kennedy, your patience and kindness make the learning process so enjoyable.
> Ms. Gallagher, you know every book by heart and provide great guidance.
> Mr. Hopkins, you make Sunrise a great place.

From my lovely Moorlands Elementary:

> Ms. McDonald, you have an encouraging and charming smile and unlocked my world of reading and writing.
> Mr. Miller, your wonderful melody of your strumming guitar enriches the learning experience.

And so many others... Thank you!

Chapter 1
FURBALL THE YOUNG MAGICORE

"EEH!" A baby fairy squealed.

"MONSTER!!! No eat baby me!"

Furball lifted up her invisible foot and looked down at the toy train, that she accidentally stepped on.

It was in pieces.

"I'm so sorry! I'll um…" Furball stuttered.

But the baby fairy's mother rushed over, snatched her son, and fled for the nearest house, looking back at Furball with anxiety in her eyes, fearing Furball would eat her baby.

The rest of the villagers banded together and quickly grabbed spears, surrounding Furball the young Magicore in a circle of defense, as if the Magicore would attack them any second.

"Leave, Magicore!" A scowling fairyman wearing dark blue stepped forward, behind him rows of fairy villagers holding spears.

"You don't belong here!" Another fairy stepped forward. She had stylish blue patterns on her hand, and her red hair was wet and dripping, with her hand on her hip.

"As if a Magicore would ever fit in." she sneered, and a bubble of water formed on her hand, the water filled with dirty salt specks and some seaweed. "Too bad you're not going to last!"

Furball backed up and prepared to run.

She knew the villagers would not take pity because she was a Magicore.

A Magicore is a magical creature with four invisible paws, making it look like an odd floating white blob with a black line across its forehead.

But her strange look wasn't the only reason that the villagers were afraid of her.

The reason was worse.

Historically, for a long time, Magicores were bad. Very bad. They attacked fairies. They did that because they were under the spell of the Bonzo flower pollen.

Being controlled by the evil spell, they had stamped through entire villages and destroyed crops and years of hard work. They also had demolished huts and fairy houses.

But when the legendary Moondust mine had been unlocked by Pia the Pinena fairy*, the breeze carried the Moondust out to the world. The Moondust spread onto Magicores, and one by one the Magicores turned back into their normal caring, loving, and exciting selves.

---

* Details of that can be found in the story "The Moondust Adventures (Pia the Pinena Fairy)" combo book. You can find it in bookstores as well as online.

Now that was a fact, but the villagers didn't believe it, still suspicious and unfriendly to Furball, who was a young Magicore.

Ouch!

Furball hit a rock behind her. That wasn't there before.

A fairy wearing brown was flying overhead using their talent to move the rocks around to form a corner, trapping Furball.

Furball trembled as tears slowly streamed down her body.

She was a Magicore, not a fairy. And she did not belong in this village full of fairies. The villagers judged her by her appearance, and also by the history of Magicores.

The villagers charged forward towards Furball.

Furball looked around.

She was trapped.

She shrunk back into the rock wall to try to hide.

Closing her eyes, she braced herself as she was shaken violently by the villagers in a flurry of hands.

A hammer flew overhead and hit her, making her blood turn cold.

Is it that hard not to be judged by one's appearance and past?

Furball wondered in agony.

Chapter 2

THE STARES OF THE VILLAGERS

"Wake up! Furball!"

A familiar voice yelled and Furball was shaken again.

Furball suddenly felt wet all over.

"No, that's enough water."

"She doesn't look very awake. Should I try more?"

Not wanting to be hit with cold water, Furball quickly opened her eyes, and glanced around the room.

She saw her roommates Pia the Pinena Fairy standing over her.

Pinena means "traveler fairy." Pia liked to solve problems and mysteries by having adventures, and gaining new knowledge from new friends she made during the travel.

Furball's bird friends Bella and Harmonica stood beside her, and Harmonica was holding a bucket of water.

"Are you okay?" asked Pia, her wings down by her side.

"You were squirming and trembling like crazy and apologizing for breaking something."

"It was just a dream?" Furball asked herself, feeling more relaxed.

"It felt so real." She recalled the rows of spears, and the disgusted look on the fairyman's face when he looked at her.

"Were you dreaming of that same dream?" Pia asked, her face was creased with concern and she was wearing a nightdress.

"Yes," Furball muttered angrily. "I said sorry but the villagers still charged at me! I just can't get away from this dream! Is it really going to happen?" her eyes widened and she held her breath.

Pia had a faraway look on her face.

"We have to do something." Pia murmured to herself.

Ever since Furball had decided to move to Pia's hometown village with their other best, best, friends, Furball had felt very uncomfortable under the stares of other fairies there.

Whenever she passed through the town, Furball could hear whispers and feel stares coming from all over the place.

She didn't like it.

Not one bit.

She had already told Pia about it, and Pia had to keep comforting everyone that Furball was no harm to them whenever the villagers complained.

But no matter how many times they tried, nobody listened.

Furball had to just grow into the habit of ignoring it. But that didn't mean Furball didn't hear what they said, or see what they did. She had feelings, too!

Furball yawned and walked down the hallway, getting ready for the day.

She stopped and peered out of the window and saw the villagers. They were shopping, picking berries, weaving grass, playing ball, and other things.

Oh, how Furball would love to join in on their games and chat with the villagers, and play ball, or pick berries with them, and help out on their farms. But that wasn't possible, for the villagers saw her as a scary Magicore.

Furball continued down the hallway and passed a mirror and paintings of fairies, and knocked on a green door with an image of many leaves posted onto it.

Moments later, a beautiful young fairy wearing a colorful yellow and purple skirt with brown-red boots appeared, thrusting open the leaf-like door. Her hair was braided with fresh flowers that matched her sparkling ember eyes.

Her wings were tinted rosy pink on the edges, and she had a brown leather belt that had a knife case with a few secret pouches for storing stuff at her sides. Her hands were hanging, clenched, and they had a pink little bubble of magic encircling them.

PIA!

Pia gestured with her hands to the door, her usual smile, but a little bit faltered, and Furball entered Pia's room.

A blanket lay neatly folded on a loft bed, and a table and beanbag were stationed at the middle of the room. Card games and a marble Magicaw sat on a shelf in the corner.

Furball noticed a small slit at the top of the Magicaw's head, to put in coins and the village currency. A Magicaw is a type of bird that makes double and triple rainbows. They also can't help repeating themselves. They're also macaws, after all!

That was the souvenir from their hot air balloon rides during the Best bird of the Year race. The race was among many quests during their Moondust Adventures.

A rainbow rug laid underneath Furball's invisible paws and stuffed toys sat on top of a shelf with books. Craft papers were spread onto the table with glue, scissors, and a jug of glitter labeled, "Crafta's crafty glitter!" on the second line it said "Sticks everywhere! Even on your wings!"

"We have to do something." Pia paced around as Furball sat down.

"Sooner or later the villagers will get tired of you. They will try to drive you out. You can't let that happen, Furball." Pia squeezed a beanie bag that said, "Friendship Forever!" And she threw it down in frustration.

Furball shivered at the thought of her haunted dream. "I know. But what can I do? I will just provoke them. They don't have any trust in Magicores. They are also very afraid. And the rumors!"

Pia hung her head. "Rainia and her twin brother Shark. Fairy of shallow and fairy of deep-water animals. They don't like you, Furball. They don't trust you."

"Yes." Furball gulped. "They are the ones who spread the rumor. They can convince the villagers to attack me and drive me out!"

"Not just them," Pia slammed her fist onto a pillow. "Anyone can. It's too easy! But the reason I suspect them is because they already hate you, the most. And they're never afraid to speak up to cause mayhem and trouble! Other than water-talent fairies, I think they should be trouble talent fairies!"

"Okay!" Pia let go of her beanie. "So, time for the good news! You can earn the villager's trust back if you pass the three tests of the Legendary Judges of Magic!"

"Legendary Judges of Magic?" Furball wondered. "How will that earn back the villager's trust?"

"The villagers judge you because of your appearance, and past of Magicores. But the villagers greatly respect the Legendary Judges of Magic. If they learn from the Legendary Judges of Magic, they might change their way of judging you." Pia told Furball.

"I heard the Judges will judge you in your good traits, Positivity, Honesty, Wisdom, Braveness and Confidence."

Pia frowned. "A little catch, though. Bad news, if you fail, you'll be kicked out of the village because the twins of trouble will succeed!" She leaned closer. "I call Rainia and Shark the Twins of Trouble. Other things you need to know about them-" Pia whipped out a list and handed it to Furball.

Looked like Pia didn't like the twins so much, she even had a list about their past trouble makings!

"Shark is one minute older than Rainia, so he kind of controls Rainia by telling her what to do. Shark has a snarky attitude, so his favorite creature is a shark. As for Rainia, she cheats, lies, and loves electric eels. They do whatever they can to get their way. Yeah, their talents were kind of obvious. They love water, all kinds. Even trouble making whirlpools! But some fairies think the twins love trouble more and that should be their talent." Furball read, and sighed, turning to Pia.

Pia groaned, unbraiding her hair and taking out the flowers in frustration. "The Twins of Trouble are bad. They also play pranks and stuff. They stir up any trouble they can find and even destroy friendships! And leave the mess for someone else to repair. Last week I helped two fairies that the twins of trouble destroyed their friendship by passing rumors and lies about them."

Being a friendship fairy, it was obvious that Pia didn't like the twins.

But again, from her description, who would? Furball wondered.

Furball raised an invisible front paw. "Hey, um, anyone going with me on the adventure to find the Legendary Judges of Magic?"

"Yes," Pia exclaimed, brightening a little. "Sapphire, Me, Harmonica, and Bella."

Sapphire was the only other fairy friend that Furball had. Furball smiled when she thought about her friend.

Furball knew the reason that Sapphire had decided to come on the adventure. She was the only one in her age group who didn't have talent yet.

Sapphire had complained many times that she really wanted to find her talent.

The adventure probably would have appeared to her as a chance to find her talent to get new skills. Furball knew the villagers also treated Sapphire differently.

Just because she was lagging on finding her talent, didn't mean Sapphire had to be treated differently!!!

"Yeah!" Furball cried. "Let's do this!"

The next day Furball woke up in her bed, feeling happy. The doorbell rang, and Furball rushed to it, only to collide with her friends in the hallway.

Feathers flew everywhere. Harmonica and Bella were birds who were fast in the air, making them not so agile on land.

They stumbled and fell. "Sorry," Furball panted. "I was going to answer the door!"

"Me too." murmured Bella and Harmonica. They all rubbed their foreheads.

Then, they all stood up and walked to the door together. They opened the door and found Pia standing outside, with a bag slung across her shoulders, a fairy next to her.

It was Sapphire!

She wore a short sleeve shirt, and a bracelet dangled from her wrists. She had short pants and a short skirt with a leather belt and brown wavy hair.

A pink flower hung from her hair and her wings had a tinge of blue. A pretty Sapphire gem hung from her well-embroidered necklace.

"Hi, Furball!" Sapphire called.

Sapphire was the only fairy in the village other than Pia that didn't judge Furball by her looks and the history of Magicores, and Furball and Sapphire were good friends.

"Hi Sapphire!" Furball waved back with her invisible paw.

"Come in!" Furball gestured. Pia and Sapphire stepped inside and they shut the door. The five friends started to discuss their adventure to the Legendary Judges of Magic.

"I know the route!" Pia exclaimed. "We just need to pass through a forest of monsters to get to the Magic Mountains, and climb from there to the summit. Then we will find the Magic Judges!"

"Great!" Harmonica cried.

"And I thought we might get hungry, so I brought some Precious berries!" Sapphire smiled, pulling out a sack of purple berries.

"There are many types of berries around, but I decided to bring Precious berries just in case. My least favorite berry would be the Nettle berries. Their bushes can't be pulled out of the ground, and they taste bad."

"What does the Nettle berries look like?" Furball asked curiously, her eyes wide as lightbulbs.

"They are green with yellow speckles. But if you see one, don't eat it!" Sapphire exclaimed. "Many animals and creatures hate it so much, they barf, spit, or even faint when they taste it!"

"That's one strong berry!" Bella butted into their conversation. "I hope any unsuspecting animal doesn't accidentally eat it!"

"Seems like you know so much about berries!" Furball's eyes widened as she asked Sapphire. "Where did you learn all about berries?"

"Um…. I don't know! I just know!" Sapphire looked confused. "It's in my memory somehow! And I don't think anybody told me about them!"

"Enough talk about berries." Pia shouldered through them, eyes bright. "Let's go!"

Chapter 3
A FOREST OF MONSTERS

OW!

Furball's invisible paws ached as she stepped on some sharp stones and she looked around.

It had been a while since they had started into the forest, going deeper and deeper, winding around gnarled tree roots or out in the open space.

Furball glanced at Sapphire and smiled. She knew that Sapphire couldn't wait to find her talent. Furball hoped that Sapphire would be successful, and herself too.

Waves of sympathy flowed from Furball and wrapped around Sapphire. Furball knew what it was like to be the only one who didn't have their talent or be an outsider. But now all that was going to change, and Furball would be judged by the Legendary Judges of Magic, and she would try her best to succeed.

Another thought drifted into her mind. What if she failed the three tests? What would happen? Would she be kicked out of the village? Or worse?

Suddenly, Furball noticed that everything was silent.

Crack!

Furball stepped on a twig. Ahead of her, Bella and Harmonica whirled around.

"SSSHH!" Harmonica whispered. They were all spread out, Furball in the middle and Sapphire in the back.

"Sorry!" Furball murmured.

"It's too quiet," Sapphire muttered a little way behind Furball. She eyed the trees warily, as if any second a monster would jump out. "Something's wrong. Very wrong."

Suddenly, a shadow jumped over them! A giant scorpion landed on the ground, making dust and dirt fly.

Its bloody red eyes narrowed to slits, and it clicked its gleaming razor claws menacingly. At the same time, its large, scaly tail waved from side to side wildly, and the stinger was shiny with venom. Its mouth was foaming over with soapy bubbles and the legs made stamps in the earth. The scorpion's eyes fixed onto Sapphire, and a claw struck the earth a needle away from Sapphire's foot.

The scorpion let out an enraged howl that pierced the air and it struck the ground like a miner digging for gold.

It knocked Sapphire off her feet.

Furball rushed to her side and defended Sapphire, pretending that she

knew martial arts trying to scare the scorpion.

"Hi-yah?!" Furball yelled.

"Martial arts stuff! Back off beast, or I will turn my full power on you!?!"

"Not going to work." Sapphire cried.

The two friends sprinted backward and their hands found sticks as a weapon to defend themselves.

The scorpion's claws pinched and made a threatening click-click clamoring. It repeatedly struck at Furball and Sapphire and they hit back with sticks, while dodging the claws.

Sapphire tried to make a water bubble to protect themselves and distract the scorpion while they ran for it. But the scorpion absorbed it with a blink of its bloody eyes.

The scorpion lunged for Sapphire, and Furball quickly kicked the scorpion, turning its attention onto Furball.

Furball gulped.

Suddenly, Pia flew down and bashed the scorpion on its head. She grabbed a stick, and began tap-dancing on the back of the scorpion, wildly making it angrily annoyed while Sapphire got the chance to escape.

"Furball!" Pia cried, while stamping on a flailing scorpion claw and waving her tap dance hat. "I'll help Sapphire take care of this scorpion. You go and warn Bella and Harmonica about the Sucker!"

"What?"

"The grass they are walking onto. It's not grass! It's fur! There is a Sucker! No time to explain! Hurry!"

"Got it!" Furball didn't know what a Sucker was but she took off like a shot, dodging trees and bushes.

She soon stumbled over a bush with purple berries, in an attempt to dodge a tree, and she instead shot straight into another bush with green berries that were speckled yellow.

Stumbling, Furball tried to get out, but she was stuck.

"Stop! Harmonica! Bella! Come back!" Furball yelled at the top of her lungs but Bella and Harmonica were too far in front and they didn't hear her warning calls.

Furball could hear nothing but the thump, thump, thumping of her heart as she repeatedly screamed.

Suddenly, Furball noticed out of the corner of her eye that Sapphire was flying in the air trying to distract the scorpion while Pia launched rocks and sticks at the scorpion.

With a swift swing of its tail, the scorpion sent Pia flying, and she landed in a bush, getting tangled.

The scorpion whacked Sapphire and she fell onto a tree stump surrounded by tall rocks.

The scorpion approached Sapphire.

Its evil gaze was locked onto Sapphire.

The scorpion's ugly gnarled mouth clamped together and twisted into an evil smile, as if it was telling Sapphire that it was time to say goodbye to the world.

Suddenly, the yellow patch of grass fur lifted up in front of Furball, knocking Harmonica and Bella off. They caught themselves mid-air flapping their wings just as an orange blob appeared.

A gap opened.

It was the mouth of the Sucker!!!

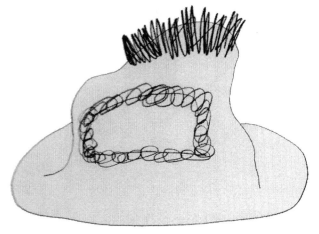

The orange blob rose up and bellowed angrily. Yellow patches of fur were placed on the top of the head, and as the Sucker swerved around, orange goo and glop oozed down its side.

Furball felt herself being tugged towards the creature and realized that it was sucking anything it saw - trees, animals, and maybe even monsters!?!

Monsters rampaged out of their hiding spots, as leaves were sucked away and dirt flew in the air.

Wind whooshed past into the Sucker's blobby mouth.

Whoosh!

Whoosh!

Whoosh!

Furball looked back towards Sapphire and the scorpion. The scorpion was about to strike Sapphire again...

At that moment, the Sucker had turned its full power onto the scorpion and the two monsters fought.

The scorpion dug its pinchers and claws into the earth, but was still sucked backward. Earth and dirt scraped by the scorpion's claws as it desperately tried to get a hold of something. Its tail tried to aim for the Sucker, though the wind was too strong and its poisonous stinger impaled itself.

A wild look flared in the scorpion's eyes before it whirled in the air.

The scorpion's legs and pinchers waved crazily and it let out an ear-piercing shriek and disappeared into the Sucker's mouth, along with other bits of debris and dirt still clutched in its claws.

As she glanced into the dark, murky, depths of the Sucker, Furball shuddered as she imaged any of her friends being in there.

Dark, cold, and in despair.

Wondering if they'd ever find the way out again to the light.

Missing their close friends and family.

Heartbroken.

And the worst of all.

Giving up on hope.

The orange goo was oozing down the Sucker as it sucked many trees, animals, including poor bunnies nibbling on carrots, eyes wide open as they flew all into the Sucker's mouth.

"No," Furball whimpered as her invisible paws clenched into a ball and dug into the earth.

Pia was clutching to her bush, and Sapphire was holding onto the tree stump surrounded by rocks. Sapphire's stump was creaking, and her grip loosening.

A sack fell from her belt.

Furball knew that was the Precious berry sack, for all the berry-shaped lumps in it.

"NO!" Sapphire cried. "Our food supply!"

Harmonica and Bella were somehow sitting on the Sucker's yellow head, and they were tangled in the Sucker's fur. The Sucker ignored them.

Furball suddenly realized that the Sucker had shifted its main sucking force onto her!

It seemed to realize that picking them off one by one was easier. Thorns were preventing Furball from flying off, for the moment.

If Furball was going to die, it was to die fighting.

Furball grabbed as many sticks as she could and let them go, hoping it would get stuck in the Sucker's throat.

Furball chucked more things at the Sucker, and soon couldn't find any other sticks or rocks.

The Sucker was closer to Furball now.

The sucking became more intensified with every gloppy step of the Sucker.

Furball was hanging onto the edge of the bush.

It would be any second now…

Suddenly, Furball noticed that the bush she was dangling onto was a Nettle berry bush.

Green berries that were speckled yellow lined the rims of the bush.

Sapphire's words came back to her.

"All creatures hate Nettle berries so much…"

Hmm.

Ding!

Light-bulb!

Furball plucked as many Nettle Berries as she could, and because the Sucker's main power was on her, she just simply let go of the berries and they whirled into the Sucker's open mouth.

It gagged a few times, not meaning to swallow the berries.

The Sucker took a few steps wonkily.

The Nettle berries were too strong for the horrible Sucker!

The Sucker fainted!!!

It was lying on the ground, all parts of it still.

"Yay! Furball!" All her friends rushed to her, Harmonica and Bella covered with the Sucker's fur.

Hugging and smiling, Pia walked up to her.

"Furball, you are so clever! How did you do that?" Pia's ember brown eyes twinkled.

Furball smiled and looked down at her own fur, all green with Nettle berries.

"Nettle Berries! I remember Sapphire saying that all the animals hated them." Furball exclaimed, jumping up and turning to Sapphire.

"Sapphire told us about the berries, and also Nettle Berries, how some creatures will faint if eaten them! So, I fed the Sucker Nettle berries, and it fainted in disgust! It's thanks to Sapphire that we're all here!"

And the next thing Sapphire did was blush like a rose, as Pia smiled and hugged Sapphire.

At the same time, Pia wondered about Sapphire's talent would be. Sapphire had gone through so much. Pia hoped that Sapphire's talent would reveal soon.

Chapter 4

MAGIC MOUNTAINS

After the Sucker incident, Pia and her friends were more cautious.

At the same time, Furball was confused.

In her old forest, it was safe, and the only danger was the vultures, but not to Furball. Magicores could take the powers of the luring vultures, so her old forest was perfectly safe with Furball.

Then she shook her head.

This was the Forest of Monsters, so you expected to have monsters in it. The name said it.

Duh.

Furball spotted a log and walked over to sit on it.

But before Furball reached it, the log shook and the wood was lifted up into the air!

It was supported by four branches as arms.

A face sprouted out of the log.

Its teeth bared, nostrils flaring.

It growled loudly.

Its breath smelled like dirt and flies.

It leaned forward to Furball as her friends rushed to her sides.

Lifting up one towering leg, the wood log tried to stamp onto Furball and her friends.

When they dodged, the animal leaned its face down and gazed into Furball's eyes and gave a hiss, sending wood specks all over the place.

Its spiky wooden fur was standing on its ends, and its teeth exposed into needles.

"Wood cat," Pia whispered. "Don't bother them when they are sleeping, they can squash you, or send splinters that can really hurt."

The wooden cat growled and flicked its tail, nearly knocking over nearby trees.

"Ouch. Splinter!" Furball plucked at an annoying splinter on her front as soon as the wooden cat was out of earshot.

Pia fastened her gaze on Furball, her brown ember eyes glittering with amusement. "Look up."

Furball looked up to find a mountain behind her. It was tall and majestic, and eagles squawked overhead.

Furball gulped as the setting sun lit up the birds as they flew off to what happened to be an eagle nest.

A full-grown eagle flew in circles overhead. The setting sun illuminated strong claws, a sharp beak, and powerful wings.

The eagle finally settled in its nest, as Furball watched. A rock dropped into her belly.

Yikes!

Eagles!

Furball knew that eagles gave no mercy. If they were hunted by the eagles, that would be bad.

Eagles had excellent eyesight, and were great hunters. When spotting their prey, they would stalk it until the last second. Then they would dive at swift speeds, their talons retracting into battle mode, hitting the target.

Pia noticed the setting sun too, for she gathered the group closer.

"It's getting dark," she announced. "We need to find shelter and food. The night will be cold, and we need something to fill our tummies and warm us up, along with a good place to stay."

"Reasonable," Harmonica noted, smoothing down her feathers stylizing.

Sapphire was still upset that she'd lost their food supply to the Sucker, and Furball bounded over to comfort her.

"You can help," she whispered. "There are other berries."

"We can use Milk berries as a food supply!" Sapphire exclaimed. "They are the tastiest berries on the Magic Mountains!" The girls cheered.

"We can split up into groups to find Milk berries!" Bella suggested.

"Yeah!" Furball cried. "And that old oak tree over there is hollow, big enough for us all! We can make some camp there!"

They split up into two groups and headed in opposite directions. Furball and Sapphire headed towards the mountains and the others went back towards the trees.

Furball shivered at walking towards the Magic Mountains.

She didn't like the eagles!

"Don't worry," Sapphire assured her, hovering beside her. Her wings fluttered rhythmically. "The eagles should be asleep by now. Plus, eagles usually don't come down here, anyway." Her words helped, but Furball was still uneasy.

What if the eagles woke up?

Sapphire leaned down to pick a milky white berry on a bush close to them. She inspected it and tossed it into a dip in the ground.

"Why did you do that?" Furball asked.

"So, we can make a pile of Milk berries instead of just holding in our hands." She glanced at Furball's invisible paws. "Or invisible paws! And we can wash the berries with water bubbles afterward, if they get dirty." She added, seeing Furball's expression of dirt on berries.

"Okay." Reasoned Furball. Then she darted forward to a bush with milky white berries. "So... Are these Milk berries?"

Sapphire inspected them. "Yes. Berries that have a creamy milk texture, okay?" Furball nodded and they picked more berries. Time flew by, and they began to leave, Sapphire made a water bubble to hold the berries for them.

Sapphire talked about berries, her favorite type, and how she first gulped down a Frost berry by accident, how she thought her insides were going to freeze, her bellyache because of it, and how Pia had made her feel better by making her some soothing tea.

She blabbed about berries and how Milk berries looked like the cold Frost berries, except with that warm feeling and tinge.

Furball commented that she had never tasted a Milk berry before, and was looking forward to, after Sapphire had described the milky sensation when you ate it, how tasty it was, and other awesome facts about Milk berries.

While Sapphire droned on about berries, Furball thought to herself.

The thought of meeting the Legendary Judges of Magic wandered into Furball's mind, and she couldn't help but get worried.

What traits did they judge by, and was she worthy enough?

They soon reached the camping spot, and Sapphire shut her mouth. The others soon got back, and they washed their berries in warm water, and Furball bit into her pile.

She and Sapphire had brought back the most berries and Furball was glad there was enough for tomorrow to eat because of that.

As she bit into her berry, a warm tinge came over her, relaxing her as she chewed onto the creamy core.

It felt relaxing after the Sucker incident, and the worry about eagles.

Straying from the small camp, Furball found a pile of rocks a little farther from the sheltering branches that hung above, and walked over, looking around into the quiet night.

Drip.

Furball whirled around and saw that water was leaking down onto a bare spot on the cold ground.

She licked her lips. She was thirsty, and that water looked clean enough, and she didn't want to wake Pia to ask for water.

How would she stop the water from washing away before she would be able to get even one sip?

Hmm.

Rocks. Pile?

Ding!

Lightbulb!

Furball nosed the pile of rocks over and made a small dam to hold the water for drinking.

Satisfied, she lapped up a mouthful and crept back to the makeshift camp to sleep with the others.

Chapter 5
A Warning Wake-up Call

WHOOO!

Furball woke up to the sound of an animal. Turning over, she wondered why the ground wasn't fuzzy and soft like her bed. It was stone cold.

Then she realized that she was in a makeshift camp, with her friends sleeping soundly.

After all that had happened, all they went through in order to get to the Legendary Judges of Magic, they must be glad to be sound asleep.

WHOOO! A screech split the air, and Furball's friends woke up.

"What?" asked Harmonica. "What's happening?" Her words were cut off by another loud screech.

Suddenly, a bald eagle dove straight towards the group, aiming for Sapphire.

Sapphire looked up just as talons gripped her sides and the eagle carried her off, with arms pinned to her hip.

Sapphire screamed as she was carried into the air.

"Sapphire!!!" Furball yelled and leaped up into the air to reach out for her friend.

Her invisible paws grasped nothing but air, and a loud wailing noise sounded around her.

Everyone stumbled out of the camp, and looked around for Sapphire.

Landing squarely on her hind paws, Furball looked around for the one who had wailed - until she realized it was coming from her own mouth.

She shut her mouth and ran after Sapphire, who was desperately screaming for help.

Sapphire was courageously pounding and kicking onto the eagle's talons, struggling as much as she could.

The thought of the eagle carrying off Sapphire to its nest and feasting her there gave Furball chills spreading rapidly throughout her body.

The rest of Furball's friends were flying behind the eagle. But wind from the eagle's strong wings was too strong for them.

They couldn't reach Sapphire!

Furball would lose one of her best friends forever!

She couldn't let that happen!

Furball's heart dropped.

WAIT!

Persistently and bravely, Pia was flying closer and closer to Sapphire. She extended her hand, hot on the eagle's trail, and reached for Sapphire's hand.

They were so close...

Pia was knocked off course by a sudden flap of the eagle's powerful wings.

She plummeted into the ground on her side. Her left wing was jerking at an awkward angle. Pain covered her face and she wailed in agony, hardly able to move a muscle.

NO!

Furball scrambled to help Pia.

On the way, she tripped over a hairy branch, her face looking anxiously to the sky.

GRRR!

A strange growling noise sounded in Furball's ears.

The branch was lifted, and Furball saw herself looking into the looming eyes of a creature half bull, and half frog.

Hmm?

Ah!

Bullfrog!!!

Furball stumbled to the ground and ran, screaming for help but never receiving any.

With a grunt, the fat Bullfrog chased her, but it must have been hard, with the legs of the frog and a bull mixed together.

The Bullfrog growled, nostrils flaring and teeth snapping.

But he was gaining on Furball fast.

Furball had to do something or she would become a pancake, squished flat. Maybe he'd add maple syrup!

Oh dear.

Furball didn't want to be his next meal!

She looked forward and realized that the eagle and Sapphire were flying towards them.

If she could turn it to her advantage!

Hmm....

Ding!

Lightbulb!

Furball stopped abruptly, and jumped onto the Bullfrog's nose. The surprised Bullfrog shook her, and was finally rearing onto his wobbling hind frog legs.

Furball bunched her invisible paws, and jumped!

With perfect aiming, she wound up onto the Eagle's back!

She reached an invisible paw out to Sapphire and pulled her out of the eagle's grasp.

Sapphire held on tight to the eagle, while Furball twisted the eagle's wings to aim at the Bullfrog. Sapphire pulled a few tail feathers ... and the eagle screeched and took off like a rocket, hitting the target.

The Bullfrog leaped back, stunned, and its cheek bruised badly. After a moment's hesitation, it's gaze locked onto the eagle. It dove at it, and soon the two animals were fighting like two two-year-old's.

Sapphire and Furball took the chance and leaped off the eagle's back.

Sapphire grasped Furball and landed on the ground.

The two friends clapped hand in paw exclaiming, "Teamwork Style!!!"

Neither Bullfrog nor Eagle noticed them, they were too busy fighting each other.

Furball and Sapphire grouped with the rest of their friends, and they escaped safely.

Furball and Sapphire's Teamwork saved the day!!!

Chapter 6

SAPPHIRE'S RELAXING MIXTURE

"Thank you for saving me!" Sapphire hugged Furball and Furball felt the warmth spread through her, warming her from top to bottom all over.

Furball hugged back.

"It was teamwork that helped us defeat the Bullfrog and Eagle!"

Then they headed towards the others. Furball tramped on all fours, and Sapphire flew quickly.

Pia was limping badly on her wing, supported by Bella and Harmonica, and they all had bruises and scratches from the fight.

They gathered together and entered a hollow oak tree. They were hurt and very tired and dirty.

Sapphire headed out and returned carrying plants, flowers, a rock, leaves, berries, and roots of plants.

Setting down three big leaves, she laid a pink flower on one and began picking off all the petals. Then she ripped them to shreds and added a spicy-smelling leaf.

"Mint," she explained when Furball asked. "It relaxes your body and makes your injuries hurt less. This pink flower is a Pollita. It will mend cuts." She crushed them with her rock and added water from her water bubble.

Then she grabbed a green berry, speckled yellow. "Nettle berries make sure the lotion and mixture stay on. They may taste bad, but they are very important in all lotions." Sapphire told Furball.

Walking over to Pia, she smeared her mixture across Pia's torn wing and wrapped it in a bandage of leaves. Pia winced at the jolt of sudden ease, said thanks, and then soon fell asleep.

Sapphire returned to Furball's side and grabbed another leaf to use as a bowl. This time she added Pollita, Mint, Daffodil juice, ten drops of water, and Grass root.

"Grass root is tasty and will stop the mixture from becoming watery, and Daffodil juice will prevent dirt from getting inside your cut." said Sapphire.

After that, Sapphire mushed it with the rock, and applied some to everyone's cuts and bruises, Furball helping, and Sapphire advised them to let it dry, and then applied some to herself.

"You are good at this," said Furball. Sapphire brought up a Nettle berry squished it, and added it to everyone's cuts again. "you should do it more often. I never seen you do this in the village."

Sapphire blushed and turned around, her eyes locking onto Furball's. "Thanks, but you should get some rest. You'll need it." Her gentle voice soothed.

Chapter 7
CHURNING RIVER

After a good rest, during which Sapphire had checked everyone at least a million times with her herbs, everyone was back on their feet.

Furball was jumping in her fur. She bounced around.

"Let's go, let's go, let's go!" She exclaimed. Sapphire smiled, amused.

"Keep jumping, and you'll be a rabbit!"

"Keep laughing and you'll be a clown!" Furball retorted, laughing herself.

Sapphire laughed too, and then they both gazed up wistfully to the early afternoon sun. "So peaceful," sighed Furball, taking it all in.

Suddenly, the crack of a twig and a complaint about too noisy twigs told Furball that she'd spoken too early.

"Let's go!" Pia stood behind Furball, supported by Bella and Harmonica dusting her feathers off.

"You should rest more, Pia." Sapphire stood up from the pile of moss that Furball and she had collected.

"No." Insisted Pia, sounding like a pouting preschooler. "I am absolutely fine."

Sapphire raised one eyebrow, starting to sound like Pia's mother or teacher. "Fine. Be careful, then. I might not have my eye on you the whole time, but I do now."

They marched up a rocky path up the mountain. Harmonica and Bella were carefully stepping over rocks in the path. As birds, they weren't used to walking, and went very slow.

Once in the Magic Mountains, you could not fly.

There were powerful winds that blew you away or back to the bottom of the mountain if you flew.

Furball didn't feel any cold air until they reached the middle. She tripped over a rock, not watching where she was going, and was swept off her feet by the strong gales of wind.

She screamed as she whirled around in the air, and Sapphire quickly pulled her back down.

"That," chattered Pia, sounding stiff as a robot. "is the reason why we do not fly! For we will be blown away by the powerful magic gales of Magic Mountain!"

Pia and Sapphire's noses were both pink from the cold, and as well for Furball - her nose was always pink.

They walked on and on until Furball thought the mountain was going on forever, did they stop.

Furball looked around for a rock to rest on for at least two seconds, but only saw a swirling river in front of her.

The river was misted along the edges and looked as it held many whirlpools. And, it probably did.

"Churning river," said Pia. "the river that is never calm, even for one second. Don't fall in. It leads to a waterfall if you don't get stuck in one of the whirlpools."

Carefully and cautiously, the group stepped over some stepping stones covered with slimy green algae, and not a single fish nor creature in sight. Only dead fish lay on the banks.

The wind was howling even harder than ever!!!

Bella was the last one to cross.

She was almost across the river…

When suddenly a wave blasted at her, and she fell into the Churning river.

Bella scrambled up, but a bone chilling cold wave overcame her and pulled her under.

Bella screeched, and bubbles popped onto the surface.

Furball darted forward and caught Bella, but was slipping rapidly in the Churning river.

"Pia, no!" Sapphire yelled as Pia caught Furball. "You're not strong enough!" She reached out to grab Pia. "Let me pull!"

"I'm not letting go!" Yelled Pia.

Suddenly, another wave rushed over and Furball and Pia PLUNGED into the Churning river.

Freezing dirty water fled into Furball's mouth and she spat it back out, trying to find air.

Which way was up?

She tumbled in the water like a lost scrap of dirt.

Furball felt like spewing her insides out.

She paddled towards anywhere, somewhere, trying to find the surface.

Her lungs scorched, and her throat tightened.

Pain seared through her.

Air… Furball needed air!

She opened her eyes in the water. They stung, and she shut them fiercely, paddling.

She could hear Sapphire and Harmonica's yells, but couldn't answer them, or she would swallow more water.

A body collided with hers.

Pia!

Furball grabbed Pia and hauled her the direction she thought was up, and her head broke the surface.

A wave crashed over her, and she took a breath before being pulled down again.

A hand and wing broke the surface above her and found their way towards Furball, helping them up. It was Sapphire and Harmonica.

There were a few yells, and Furball was pulled up along with Pia onto the surface.

But where was Bella?

Furball shook her head "I don't know" and hoped for the best. She turned to look at Pia, who was coughing up mouthfuls of dirty ice-cold water.

Pia paused a moment to say thanks to Furball, and then started coughing again.

Suddenly, Bella's head bobbed to the surface of the water. It sputtered, choked, and was swiftly blown towards the waterfall, pulled under by the rip current.

"NO!" Harmonica screamed.

"BELLA!!!! Hang on, I'll come to get you!" She attempted to dive into the water, but Furball grabbed her wing to stop her.

"What are you doing?" shrieked Harmonica. "I have to go save her! Not like there is going to be some type of magical force to hold her there!"

"Are you crazy?" cried Furball. "You don't even know how to swim!"

Wait!

Magical Force?

So many rocks…

Hmmm…

Ding!

Lightbulb!

"There is a force." cried Furball. "And we can make one." As Sapphire stared at her in confusion, Furball exclaimed, "A dam. A dam will catch Bella and stop her from falling into the waterfall. I just need someone to stop her from going towards the waterfall so fast."

Pia's hand raised, and she stood up, some water still trickling from her wings, and she coughed out the last of dirty cold water.

"Let's do it." Pia waved a hand and a bubble popped onto Bella, filled with air. Pia stuck out her arm, and kept the bubble with Bella in it in place, as waves surged towards them.

As Pia kept Bella at bay, Furball quickly instructed Sapphire and Harmonica to make a dam.

Harmonica gathered rocks and mud, and Sapphire put a water bubble around them to carry it, plopping them into the water.

After they finished one row, Sapphire applied mud to the rocks, sealing all cracks between them as Furball carefully inspected each one, filling the wholes with twigs.

No mistakes or the whole dam would burst, and their plan would be ruined.

"Hurry! I can't hold Bella much longer!" Pia groaned.

Harmonica whipped around and rushed towards Pia.

"You have to hold her, please! A bit longer!" Harmonica begged. "You can do it! I know you can!" As a reply, Pia gave a strained moan.

Furball suddenly noticed and realized that most of fairy's magic power came from their wings. Pia's wing was half-healed.

Furball ran over to Pia and picked up the bandages that had fallen from Pia's wing. She rewrapped it around Pia's wing and Harmonica helped, hearing Pia sigh that it felt better now.

Then they rushed back to the dam. Without constant care, the dam was spilling holes that would soon become bigger!

Quickly Furball found some mud and small rocks, giving them to Sapphire.

Sapphire picked out the holes and patched them. Suddenly, Pia's magic collapsed under the power of the Churning river, and Bella hurtled towards the dam.

Sapphire barely patched the last hole, just as Bella slammed into the dam.

The waves pushed against the dam.

Creak. They had to hurry, or the dam would soon burst under the weight of the water.

Harmonica grabbed a branch from a tree up high and yelled for Bella to grab it.

Bella grappled the branch tightly, and together, they pulled her out to safety.

CRASH!

The dam erupted, and the remains of it were only a small pile of rocks.

Chapter 8
TEMPLE OF MAGIC

After they had worked together to make it through the incident at the Churning river, the five friends crossed small plains, and stumbled over many rocks, along the journey.

Furball bounced on her toes to find the Legendary Judges of Magic.

The top of the Magic Mountains was within their reach.

Above, the clouds were few and bright. The sun shone brighter than all the nighttime stars, and the only hint of wind rustled the leaves of a grove of evergreens and fir trees.

The rocky mountain path extended to a wide dirt-paved road, and the grass and wildflowers beside it were as fresh as a nightingale's song.

The flowers were sweet as honey, and they covered the landscape in many rainbow patches. Daffodils. Daisies. Pansies. Sunflowers. Who knew there were such majestic flowers that seemed to bring spring to a mountain!

The sky's turquoise blue color drained onto a small pond filled with ducks and geese. Cattail stuck out from random places and lined the water's edge while Dragonflies flitted over.

The steep mountain was flatter, now a large wide plain.

There were no more big gales or troubles.

Everything was peaceful. A little squirrel hopped underneath Pia, winding between her legs.

"Let's take a break." decided Pia. "Right here. We can spread out."

Only a small scar remained of Pia's torn wing.

Furball was glad she had healed, because she knew Pia felt much better, without a bandage tagging along with her.

Furball also knew that Pia was a proud fairy, with or without scars.

But Pia still left the flying to the others. Sapphire had advised Pia not to fly for at least a month, or she would take a risk of cutting her wings again.

As everyone found a spot to sleep or rest, Furball lay in the grass, listening to the squirrel's scatter, birds chirp, or sometimes she would just think of how much she wanted to be known as who she really was.

She HAD to be trusted again.

After a minute, Sapphire joined her and gazed at the flower she was holding, a flower with an orange ring inside and then followed by more rings of color, blue, red, green, and pink.

Furball heard her whisper, "So rare." To the flower and as she twirled it around her thumb.

They laid in the grass for a while in silence.

Furball needed to find the Legendary Judges of Magic, and she opened her eyes wide.

Furball sat up and saw that the others were dozing lightly. "Come on," she nudged Sapphire. "Let's explore."

Sapphire sat up. "Well, maybe, for a little while." And they set off, smiling at the bunnies, or stopping to pick pretty flowers.

Time ticked by, and Furball found herself having so much fun exploring nature and picking flowers.

Nature was fun and beautiful!

Suddenly she spotted a small trail of rainbow flowers, the type Sapphire had weaved into a bracelet.

"What?" asked Sapphire when Furball pointed. "What? Oh! The trail! Rainbow Ringed flowers! They are rare, but why are there so many there?"

Dropping the flowers in their hand, Furball and Sapphire followed the Rainbow Ringed flowers.

They lifted up large brambles in the path and peered under.

Sunlight filtered through the brambles ahead and illuminated the clearing.

A rainbow crossed the sky and butterflies filtered in the distance. Rows and rows of colorful plants, flowers, and berries were rooted to the ground.

They were so busy smelling the scents of flowers, that they didn't notice a temple in the distance.

A butterfly landed on Furball's nose and she followed it, spinning around.

Suddenly, Furball saw the temple.

The temple was looming, and ancient looking. Vines draped the roof, and stone marble pillars supported it.

Furball nudged Sapphire, and glanced towards the temple.

Sapphire was still rolling in the flowers, but she got up and gave Furball a questioning look. "What is it?"

"There." Furball pointed to the temple.

And without another word, Furball tore towards the temple…

"FURBALL! SAPPHIRE!" a voice called. "Where are you?"

Furball whipped around as Pia, Harmonica, and Bella emerged from the undergrowth brambles.

"PIA! Look! I found a temple there!!!" Furball yelled excitedly, bouncing up and down. She motioned behind her.

"WOW! The meadow!" Pia, Harmonica, and Bella exclaimed.

"WOW! What a temple!" This time Sapphire joined in.

Then Pia ran towards the Temple, and stopped by Furball, taking it in.

"The Temple of Magic!" Pia cried, eyes as big as golfers. "It was here all along!"

She put her hands on Furball's paws. "Furball, you know what you did?" Pia cried as the others came over.

"You found the Temple of Magic!"

Chapter 9
LEGENDARY JUDGES OF MAGIC

"Yes, you did." A silky voice purred.

"You found the Temple of Magic."

Another voice interrupted the first. "Well, it was just behind them, Dazzle!" the stout voice persisted.

"Eh." A squeaky voice said happily.

"What are you so happy about, Piper?" the stout voice asked.

"Eh. I don't know."

"Who are you?" Harmonica demanded, her needle-sharp eyes scanning the clearing.

"Show yourself!" She bunched her wings, ready to fly.

Pia fixed her gaze on the willow tree and Bella looked at the temple.

Amber eyes flashed in the shade of the willow tree Pia was staring at.

"Who I am, Darling? Me?" asked the same silky voice.

"My, my, I would ask you to be politer first, honey."

"Dazzle!" exclaimed a squeaky voice. "She's Dazzle!"

There was movement in the tree, and someone said, "That's me you're jumping on!" a "Oh, Sorry! I'll find some other place to jump on, then!" And soon enough, there was another "ow" and "sorry".

"I don't think that's a branch." Said the stout voice.

A second later, a small mouse fell from the tree.

It hit the ground with a thump and stood up, facing them.

"Hi!" It exclaimed. "I'm Piper, Legendary Judge of Magic for Positivity and Honesty!"

Furball gawked at the tiny mouse.

"What?" Piper asked. "Oh! Do you want to see the others?" and Piper called up the tree.

"Come down, Dazzle! Oh, and also Wordsearch!"

A white bundle of feathers swooped down from the tree and Furball noticed it had a beak, white feathers, a round head.... A snow owl!

"Bonjour, that's hello in French, and I'm Wordsearch. I'm the Legendary Judge of Magic for Wisdom."

Wordsearch the snow owl scanned them over with his razor-sharp eyes.

"As the famous William Shakespeare said, "To be or not to be, that is the question."' He quoted formally.

Piper bounced up and down.

"Honestly, Wordsearch, you are quite smart but boring." Piper flicked his brown tail towards the tree.

For a small brown mouse, Piper had a big mouth! "Come on down, Dazzle!"

There was a flash of brown and white and a beautiful leopard stood before them.

"I am Dazzle, the Legendary Judge of Magic for Braveness and Confidence. And we are the Legendary Judges of Magic."

Dazzle was dazzling, as the name suggested. Her leopard fur patterns were outstanding, and she had an ember glow in her eyes.

Her strong talons reflected the sunlight, and she looked like she had spent every spare second to groom herself, for her fur was flat down her spine.

Furball soon became very embarrassed, because her fur must have been sticking out to the side, which looked very awkward.

She also remembered that the Judges were supposed to Judge her, and she put on her best smile.

Pia, Furball, Sapphire, Harmonica, and Bella all bowed.

"We are very honored to meet you, oh great Legendary Judges of Magic." Pia spoke. Her voice was clear and strong.

Pia introduced themselves to the Legendary Judges of Magic, one by one.

"At ease." Dazzle smiled, and the five friends slowly got up.

She grinned and leaped onto a rock, her coat shining vibrantly.

Glancing at Sapphire, Dazzle meowed. "Don't be afraid to ever speak up or do something new."

The rock she was standing on was levitated, and she disappeared into the Temple of Magic, Piper darted from side to side following her, and Wordsearch flew quickly and silently.

The friends followed them inside.

The Temple of Magic was dark at first when they entered, but the hallway led to a big room with a stage filled with seats.

The Magic Judges sat in the first row of seats, and Dazzle gestured for them to stand on the stage.

"You probably didn't know we have powers," Dazzle meowed. "My power is that I can become invisible, Piper can make anyone laugh, and Wordsearch knows all the quotes in the universe."

"Of course, we also have special rocks that can fly and carry passengers." She nodded to the rock right next to her.

Furball's invisible legs trembled, as Dazzle stared at her as if reading her past.

"Furball, Sapphire. We heard about you two. And we will ask you a question." Dazzle told them, and Piper stepped forward.

"What is the reason you came here?" quizzed Piper, his bright eyes burning into Furball's.

"Well, I want to earn the trust of the villagers and I need to pass your test to do that." Furball exclaimed.

Dazzle flicked her tail. "This way." She padded along a hallway with Wordsearch and Piper, Furball following.

They went down to a door in the temple's room, and Dazzle stopped walking. "I will go back to the main temple room." She told Furball. "If you need help, Wordsearch will give you hints. Piper will test Sapphire, then if you both pass, you will do the final test."

Dazzle and Piper left, and Wordsearch nudged Furball towards the door.

"Go through this door, and you will find a small box lying on a chair in a room." Wordsearch told her.

"It will be a puzzle box. Use your surrounding objects to help you open the box." Wordsearch made motions that showed how big the box was. "When you open it, use the clue to find and then bring the gemstone to me."

A gemstone…. WOW!

Furball entered the room and looked around. In front of her, as Wordsearch had said, was the chair with the box on it.

As Furball peered closer, she saw that the box had one lock that sealed it shut. She needed to open the box... how would she do that?

First, she needed a clue, but she didn't have one. Wordsearch had told her to use the surrounding objects to help her.

Maybe the box had something to do with Wordsearch.

This box was a puzzle, and Wordsearch was the Legendary Judge of Magic of Wisdom.

Wisdom included knowledge, and probably mind teasers or puzzles. Hmm.

Where would you go to search for knowledge or learn something new? The library! It had lots of books, fiction and legends.

And you could learn from them!

Math, reading, fictional, nonfiction, and craft books were only a few varieties.

Wordsearch might have hidden it there, by the name.

It might not work, but… It didn't hurt to try!

Furball sped over to a bookshelf in the small room, and searched the books one by one. She pulled them out and flipped through the pages to try to find the key, maybe hiding in the book.

Finally, Furball found a small bronze key in a dictionary.

Hey!

Wordsearch hid the key in a dictionary, another form of a word searcher!

She pulled it out and padded to the small box, clicking it open using the key.

Furball lifted the lid and set the lock aside. Inside, was a sheet of bark with clues on it.

She read it over two times to try to mesmerize.

This is what the poem said;

A tiny, shiny, sparkling thing

Too small to see
Intensified by many and many
Looking as normal
As it was to be

Hmm.

That must mean the prize gem was tiny, hidden somewhere in the room. Gems were usually well polished and shiny, Furball thought. And especially if they're from the Legendary Judges of Magic!

But what about the last part of the poem?

Intensified by many and many
Looking as normal
As it was to be

That meant something could make the gem bigger, or at least look bigger as it was supposed to be big originally.

But where was the gem?

Maybe Furball could start looking for the tool that made the gem look bigger, and then search the room closely using it.

That could work.

Furball scanned the room. There was a box of pencils set aside on a table. A magnifying glass lay by it, and a blank piece of white bark.

The bookshelf was full of preverb books and dictionaries, and on the ground, there was the chair with the box lying on it.

LIGHTBULB!

YEAH!

Magnifying glass!

That was it!

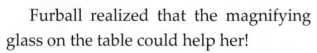

Furball realized that the magnifying glass on the table could help her!

Unlike a normal magnifying glass, magical ones had a "big" switch and "off" switch.

You would make sure the magnifying glass was "off" before looking at something through the viewer.

Then you would flick the switch, and your object you were looking at will become bigger!

YES! The magical magnifier will actually make objects bigger!

The gemstone was small, and using the magnifying glass, Furball could make it bigger!

Furball rushed to the small desk, and grabbed the magnifying glass. She looked around, her eye in the magnifying glass.

She skimmed through the desk, until her eye caught something shiny.

Furball looked closer and saw a sparkling, smooth blue gemstone!

She quickly flicked the "Big" switch on the magnifying glass, and a flash of light blinded her.

Furball opened her eyes to see the blue gemstone, now big enough to hold without losing it.

She had completed the task!

"I got IT!" Furball burst through the door, and handed the gemstone to Wordsearch, who was waiting outside.

"Excellent." Wordsearch nodded formally.

"Well done! Come, they are waiting."

He led Furball back to the Temple's main room, where Sapphire stood, a grin plastered across her face.

Furball and Sapphire exchanged news on their tests, and cheered together.

Sapphire had passed her test, about plants and retrieving a sunflower seed in the patch of poisonous ivy.

Sapphire said that she was getting grumpy and upset every time she had stepped into the poisonous ivy, and she wasn't allowed to fly, either.

Sapphire was going to give up until she remembered what Piper said, "You can do it! I know you can!"

And Sapphire had felt more positive and kept going, even if she had rashes on her legs!!!

Finally, she had made her way to the Sunflower seed, but couldn't grab it.

Sapphire had soon found out there was a forcefield around the seed that kept you from getting the Sunflower seed.

Sapphire recalled what Pia did, when she unlocked the Moondust Mine in her adventure.

So Sapphire chanted and pep-talked herself, "I can do this!" over and over, by being honest to herself and her dreams.

Magically, the forcefield disappeared, and Sapphire grabbed the seed.

And that was how Sapphire had completed her task!

"Now we will have the final test," Dazzle announced.

And she grinned. "No one has ever passed this test. "

"To pass this test, you will need to defeat... A Fire-breathing dragon"

"A Fire-breathing dragon!" Sapphire and Furball gasped.

"A Fire-breathing dragon?" Pia, Harmonica, and Bella gasped.

Harmonica fell over onto Bella, and they both collapsed in a heap behind Pia, the only one stable.

"But that is impossible!" exclaimed Sapphire. "Our greatest fairy hero could not defeat a dragon! And we're probably no better!"

"Give up? Okay, go home, fail." Dazzle meowed. "Your choice. Defeat the dragon by taking its dragon egg. Now, this is hard, so you two will work together. Are you READY?"

Sapphire turned pale, but Furball knew she couldn't back down. "We're ready!"

"Remember," Dazzle meowed. "if you give up, tell us. Don't risk your life if you find you can't do it."

Pia's face clouded. "Could you give them a bit of starter's advice?"

Wordsearch's beak opened, but Piper covered his mouth.

"Let me do it!" Piper told Wordsearch. "After all, I am the Legendary Judge of Magic for Positivity and Honesty!"

"I can give an honest advice!" Piper squeaked.

He turned to Sapphire and Furball. "Here's my advice."

"Stay Alive! Don't Die!" he exclaimed.

Furball and Sapphire's jaws dropped.

"Seriously?" Sapphire's wings stopped fluttering, and she dropped to the ground, stumbling.

"We'll keep that in mind," Furball muttered while she dragged Sapphire towards the auditorium.

"Yeah." Sapphire whimpered as they were brought into a large auditorium.

Dazzle, Wordsearch, and Piper sat in the booth along with Pia, Harmonica, and Bella.

Dazzle flicked her tail and Piper nodded and hopped on a button.

A large dragon appeared out of the iron doors, and breathed fire viciously.

Chapter 10
BATTLE OF THE DRAGON!

Furball and Sapphire entered the battle auditorium for the final task. Defeat the dragon and take its egg.

The dragon had glinting green eyes narrowed and its scales were shiny fire red. Large talons scraped the ground, creating a noise so deafening that Sapphire covered her ears.

Its spiked wings beat powerfully, creating a small gale.

Three small unicorn horns lined its nostrils. Two spikes on the dragon's head were pulled back, sharp as a blade of diamonds.

A webbed fin lined the back of the Dragon's head, stopping by the neck as the dragon let out a roar.

Pia, Harmonica, and Bella watched them in the booth with the Legendary Judges of Magic.

They held many encouraging signs, Harmonica stumbling with the weight of one.

She gave a big, loud, "Oof!" and fell over.

Pia and Bella bent down to help her, and dropped their signs.

As soon as Pia, Harmonica, and Bella weren't looking, Sapphire moaned and fell to the ground.

"Sapphire!" Furball raced over to her. "Are you okay?"

"I can't do this!" Sapphire wailed. "We're gonna get killed! Defeating a dragon is impossible! They're so big, and we're tiny! We don't stand a chance!"

She burst into sobbing tears and wiped the water with a handkerchief. Sapphire blew her nose, continuing to sob. "Furball, L-let's quit! I give up! I can't do this, the dragon is so s-scary!!!"

"You can do this," Furball told her. "Pia would find a way. Think what Pia would do."

Pia held up a rainbow decorated sign that said, "Belief! Confidence!" with rainbows and flowers on the edges.

Harmonica and Bella were huddling together, and it looked like they were preparing some sort of cheer.

"Stand up and fight?" Sapphire whimpered, answering Furball's previous comments.

"Exactly." Furball helped her up. "We're going to stand and FIGHT, Teamwork Style!"

Together they walked towards the dragon.

"BEGIN!" Dazzle yelled from the booth.

The dragon seemed to obey her, as if it had been waiting for this precious moment.

It rapidly puffed fire at Furball and Sapphire.

Sapphire flew into the air and dodged the fire shots swiftly, distracting the dragon.

Furball used this moment to stealthily creep onto the dragon's back.

She jumped from side to side, and bunched her legs, a giant leap to the head in one rapid move.

Furball pummeled the dragon, with her full power.

The dragon's eyes darted up.

It breathed fire at Furball, the fire intensified with rage.

It was so hot, Furball felt like a marshmallow, clung to the fiery heat from the dragon.

While the dragon was distracted, Sapphire flew down and grabbed the dragon's egg, her eyes fixed onto it.

The mommy dragon noticed this, and roared loudly, but it dared not breath fire in case her egg would burn.

The raging dragon followed Sapphire, who was flying fast as her wings would carry her towards the exit.

The dragon reached out a paw, talons extended, and swiped at Sapphire.

Alarmed, Sapphire looked back and crashed into the auditorium's walls.

She collapsed onto the ground below, the egg rolling out of reach.

Satisfied, the dragon lumbered over to grab her egg and Sapphire, who was limp on the ground.

"Sapphire!" Furball shrieked, still on the dragon's head.

Sapphire got up, rubbing her head and her eyes widened in shock as she saw the mommy dragon coming.

Furball yanked a few scales on the dragon and it let out a roar, shaking Furball to the ground.

Furball landed on the ground and bolted up.

She ran as fast as her legs would carry her, ignoring the searing hot pain of her hind invisible leg.

The dragon was lumbering closer, but Sapphire was trapped. The only way out?

Under the dragon.

Too late!

The dragon took its egg and snorted at Sapphire.

Behind, Sapphire could see Furball running towards her, screaming, but she wouldn't be there in time.

Pia was trying to fly down to Sapphire, but she kept smashing into the glass. Harmonica and Bella attempted to help, but they couldn't help covering their faces.

The Legendary Magic Judges were shouting at the dragon, yelling that the dragon was going too far, but the dragon didn't hear them.

Sapphire closed her eyes and braced herself as the dragon's foot came bearing down at her.

Did she die nobly?

Was she dead?

Suddenly, a magical sensation overcame her! Sapphire found herself in a magical meadow filled with flowers and plants.

Knowledge overcame her, and she breathed in the beautiful scents of the berry vines and approached a Nettle berry.

She pulled one berry off the stem and tasted it. It didn't taste as bad as she first had tried it.

In fact, as she looked into the insides of the berry, magical sparkles filled the air.

Was this a magical meadow?

Sapphire reached out and touched a vine that was curled out as if it had wanted to shake her hand.

Suddenly, everything started to disappear and fade away, and Sapphire dropped onto the dirt.

Pounding noises screeched in her head.

"Go away," Sapphire muttered, but the noises didn't stop.

She opened her eyes, a retort in her mouth. She wanted the meadow to come back!

She blinked opened her eyes and a wall of green was wrapping Sapphire's arm like a snake….

Sapphire looked around and saw vines sprouting from the bare earth and the green stuff wrapped around her arm was a berry vine.

The plants were protecting her from the dragon's clobbering foot!

It was so clear…

"I'm Sapphire, Fairy talent Growth of Berries!" Sapphire yelled. "And I can do this!"

She rolled out of the dragon's foot range and stood, raising her arm.

Immediately vines with purple berries attached broke through the earth and wrapped around one of the dragon's hind foot, securing it in place.

This is where she belonged!

Furball bounded over quickly.

Together they fought the dragon.

Together in Teamwork!

Furball distracted the dragon by nipping on its legs while Sapphire grew berry vines around the feet, one by one while the dragon wasn't watching it.

But the dragon's fire breath was too powerful, and it blew the vines to smithereens.

"Use Nettle Berry bushes!" Screamed Furball. "It's strong!"

Sapphire nodded, and using her newly found talent, curly vines formed a bush around the dragon's foot, and the berries formed neatly on the outside.

Using their other tactic, they distracted the dragon and grew more nettle berries until they finally surrounded all four feet of the fuming dragon.

Furball grabbed the egg, lying underneath the dragon's belly, and paw in hand, Furball and Sapphire passed the finish line and exit, into the temple hall.

Dazzle met them at the entrance with the other Judges and their friends.

Pia dashed over and wrapped them in a hug. "I was so worried about you!" she cried. "But you did it!!!"

Happy tears streamed down all five friend's cheeks, and they hugged once more.

"Cool!!!" cried Piper. "I'm so happy for you!"

"You did it." Said Wordsearch formally, though it looked like he couldn't help clicking his beak happily.

"Congrats." Dazzle meowed. "You are worthy. We are sorry that it almost stepped on you, Sapphire. But Dragons are Dragons, yet a bit aggressive they are. But now I must set the dragon free of the Nettle berry bush."

"But you can't break it!" Furball blurted. "It's a Nettle berry bush!"

Dazzle grinned. "Don't doubt these claws."

She bounded into the fight space and slashed at the Nettle berry vines. They came off easily, and Furball and Sapphire stared, jaw open.

Dazzle padded over as the dragon sat on the ground, making a noise that sounded like a purr.

"The mother dragon is happy that we found two worthies to raise her egg," Dazzle told them. "She wants best for her egg. That's why she fought so hard to find ones so worthy. She trusts you will take care of it. She also says it will hatch soon."

"We can keep a dragon egg!!!" Furball and Sapphire cheered and Sapphire did cartwheels in mid-air.

The egg was the color of light lavender.

Furball and Sapphire noticed an engraving of two hearts, one on each side of the egg.

They leaned close and hugged it, feeling strong beating pulses from inside, and Sapphire put her hand on the smooth glossy surface and smiled.

Chapter 11

BACK AT THE VILLAGE

Holding the Dragon Egg, Furball and Sapphire entered the Village. Pia at their side. Harmonica and Bella behind them.

The villagers became quiet.

"It's the Dragon's egg!" an old fairy cried out. "I recognize that egg! It's the last Fire Unicorn Water hybrid dragon egg in the whole universe!"

The crowd Oohed, and a few fairies swooned.

"Owned by the Legendary Judges of Magic, legend says only the worthiest ones will pass the final test and get the egg!" The librarian fairy held a book labeled "dragons."

The librarian flipped to a page and showed the crowd excitedly. The page shown an egg exactly like the one Furball and Sapphire were holding. "That species of dragon hasn't been seen for centuries!" cried the librarian.

A member of the village council stepped forward, addressing to the crowd.

"This was the final test where even our old fairy hero failed." He turned to Furball and Sapphire. "But you passed the final test of the Legendary Judges of Magic!" He declared.

"And Sapphire found her talent!" Pia joyfully cried, gesturing to Sapphire.

"Growth of Berries!" Sapphire exclaimed proudly, Furball hugging her.

Pia stepped forward, her wavy hair swishing to her side.

"We learned something very important throughout the journey."

All eyes settled on her.

"We learned that the Legendary Judges of Magic evaluate you by your traits. The traits are Positivity, Honesty, Wisdom, Braveness, and Confidence."

Pia smiled. "We also hope all the fairies and all the creatures can learn to get to know each other that way, too."

The council members looked at one another.

"That is very wise advice." Spoke the head of the council. "We agree and we will follow that advice."

"We are sorry for misunderstanding you, Furball." All the village councils and leaders walked towards Furball.

"We saw you as a scary Magicore on the outside. Not the true you on the inside."

They then nodded to Sapphire.

"Sapphire, we didn't know we were doing the opposite of helping you. You just had to believe. Sapphire, we learned an important lesson today!"

Furball noticed Shark and Rainia among the crowd that had gathered. Shark was glaring at Furball, but Rainia looked slightly ashamed when her brother wasn't looking.

"Thank you!" Furball told the council and the rest of the villagers. "Sapphire and I had to believe in ourselves to find out what to do. And we did it!"

The villagers cheered for Furball, Sapphire, and Pia, as Harmonica and Bella flew in loops overhead.

And soon all the villagers were congratulating Furball and Sapphire for their achievement.

Sapphire and Pia both raised their hands and waved, sparkles flying from their fingertips.

A "Poof!" later a huge table stood before them, piled with popsicles, ice cream, candies, cupcakes, pies, and many other delicious snacks.

Bamboo chairs lined the rim of the table, and everyone stared at it, suddenly feeling hungry.

Balloons tied to rocks sat in clumps on the ground, and confetti showered above.

"Dig in!" Pia cried, and the villagers and friends ran to get a good spot to sit in.

They feasted and Furball sat by Pia and Sapphire, munching on a cupcake.

Furball, Sapphire, and Pia smiled at each other.

Furball and Sapphire demonstrated their personalities and passed the tests of the Legendary Judges of Magic, where they were not evaluated by their appearance nor past.

They learned the importance of Wisdom, being Honest and Positive, and acting Bravely with Confidence.

And we all can do that too!

LESSONS I LEARNED FROM WRITING THIS STORY

When I was writing this story, I noticed many ways that helped me improve the story.

I want to share these lessons here in this special part of this book, hoping you will find them helpful!

Lesson 1: Bubble charts are great to help organize the story!

For example: I used the bubble chart to help me create plots and twists, like the scorpion and Sucker scenes. They helped me think deeper into the story by listing things like, settings, characters, and the main problem, with a solution.

Lesson 2: Bring characters to life by giving them emotions and personalities.

For instance: Furball is warm-hearted, but clumsy. In this story, she nearly sat on the Wooden cat and ran into trouble a lot.

On the other hand, er - invisible paw, Furball always thinks, "Lightbulb!" good humoredly before saving the day!

Lesson 3: Wear my character's shoes, so I see what the character should do.

In the battle with the dragon, I pretended I was Furball to see what I would have done, being scared but very determined. This enabled me to come up with many details and descriptions for the battle scene.

Lesson 4: Stories can be fictional, but logic must flow well.

When I finished with my first draft, I tried to revise my book. I found in the chapter "Legendary Judges of Magic" the first two tests the judges gave were too simple -- they were basically little kid rhymes.

This isn't logical because in another chapter, I mentioned that even the village's "greatest fairy hero" couldn't pass the tests. So, I rewrote the whole chapter because of that.

Lesson 5: Show, don't tell.

I found it better to show my character's emotions by describing the reactions, instead of simply saying they were sad or happy.

For example, "She couldn't let that happen! Furball's heart dropped." Furball was sad, by the action of her "heart" metaphor.

"Furball and Sapphire cheered and Sapphire did cartwheels in mid-air." This demonstrates that Furball and Sapphire were both happy, by doing cartwheels.

Lesson 6: Take away unnecessary characters.

Unnecessary characters don't contribute to the story and plot, and they sidetrack the topic.

For example: In my first draft, I introduced Pia's dad to the story. His only part was to say hi to Furball and answer the door, literally? Pia's dad could totally distract readers in these scenes, so I decided to only bring him in... later in my other books.

Lesson 7: Add funny moments in the story.

This creates memorable moments for the character and story plot.

For instance: when I was revising my book for the second time, I decided to make Piper give Furball and Sapphire *Positive* and *Honest* advice before they were going to battle against the dragon. His advice was, "Stay Alive! Don't Die!"

Lesson 8: Learn from a variety of books and Movies.

I tried my best to learn from many books and movies. That helped my writing skills especially when I wrote the battle scenes.

For example: I learned how to write intensely when I looked from both boy's and girl's perspective.

Immerse yourself in the wonderful world of
Pia the Pinena Fairy!

Pia the Pinena Fairy

The Moondust Adventures

Come and join me in this daring quest!

In the searching for my fairy talent, I rescued my mermaid friends Marissa & Emily from the spells of evil elves. I unlocked the epic Moondust mine, reversing the fate for the cursed Magicores. We evaded the crazy monkey king, and fought the vicious flock of viral vultures. Plus, I encouraged my bird friend Harmonica to build friendship with her old archenemy and they worked together to win The Best Bird of the Year contest. And the best part? During this great adventure, I found the true and MAGICAL meaning of Friendship!

Pia the Pinena Fairy
The Moondust Adventures

Combo: 2 stories in 1

By Amy Zhao

Pia the Pinena Fairy
The Legendary Judges of Magic

By Amy Zhao

100+ pages full of adventures and fun!

New! including writing tips and lessons I found that may help everyone write their own stories!

This book →

Pia the Pinena Fairy
The Legendary Judges of Magic

Now you have experienced all the adventures with Pia in this story!

Do you think you can write a review for this wonderful story? Share it with your friends, or work with your parents to share it online. When you post a review, I will be able to see it.

Thank you!
- Amy Zhao

Pia the Pinena Fairy
Saving Maui

Maui was destined to be doomed by the feared villain Slate of Chaos! However, my friends and I weren't letting Maui go down without a fight.

We embarked on a dangerous mission to save Maui, which led us into the ocean. We met friendly mermaids, but were ambushed by cursed pirates and their shadow monsters. Sacrifices were made, demons were summoned, and my friends & I battled an army of giant spiders led by Slate of Chaos himself.

But the disturbing rumor about Slate's TRUE evil plan? Oh, everyone wished it wasn't true.

But unfortunately, it was...

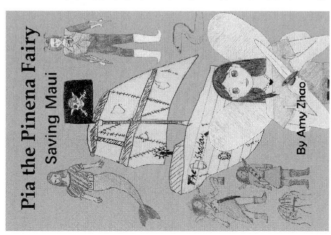

Pia the Pinena Fairy
Saving Maui

By Amy Zhao

Made in the USA
Monee, IL
28 August 2019